SAGITTARIUS
11/22-12/21

SCORPIO
10/23-11/21

LIBRA
9/23-10/22

VIRGO
8/23-9/22

LEO
7/23-8/22

CANCER
6/21-7/22

9

8

7

6

5

4

LIBRA

DECISIONS, DECISIONS

BY MICHELLE TEA   ILLUSTRATED BY MIKE PERRY

dottir press

NEW YORK CITY

Published in 2019 by Dottir Press
33 Fifth Avenue
New York, NY 10003

Dottirpress.com

FIRST EDITION
First printing September 2019

Production by Drew Stevens

Trade distribution by Consortium Book Sales and Distribution, www.cbsd.com. For inquiries about bulk sales, please contact jb@dottirpress.com.

Library of Congress Cataloging-in-Publication Data is available for this title.
ISBN 978-1-9483-4014-4

Manufactured in Canada by The Prolific Group, 2019

IN MEMORY OF ALEXIS PERSYKO,
THE FINEST LIBRA WHO EVER SAMPLED THIS EARTH,
FOUND IT BEAUTIFUL, AND SHARED THAT BEAUTY.
—MT (AQUARIUS)

LUCKY FOR ME, LIBRAS ARE SOME OF MY CLOSEST FRIENDS.
I AM ESPECIALLY GRATEFUL TO J BELL,
WHO BRINGS BALANCE DAILY.
—MP (CANCER)

I am Libra, the Scales.
Also known as the Fair-Minded
and Just.
I like to keep things balanced and equal
to harmonize the vibes.
I never cause a
fuss.

I like to let people know they are appreciated. Handwritten notes are so heartfelt.

By helping people see both sides, I can heal arguments.

All Libras are born in the fall, between September 23rd and October 22nd. The earth is transforming all around us, blazing with colors.

The sweet chill in the air makes us want to get all snuggly and cozy. It's almost time for Halloween!

Yesterday I was on my way to a French pastry shop that sells the finest mille-feuille in town, when I ran into my friend Scorpio.

Hey Libra, I'm just getting my decorations for my big Halloween party. It's going to be the spookiest, sparkliest, most haunted and cobwebby Halloween party ever!

Goth means dressing up fancy AND spooky! Black lace and big hair like a tarantula! Makeup like a vampire! Crystal jewelry like a witch!

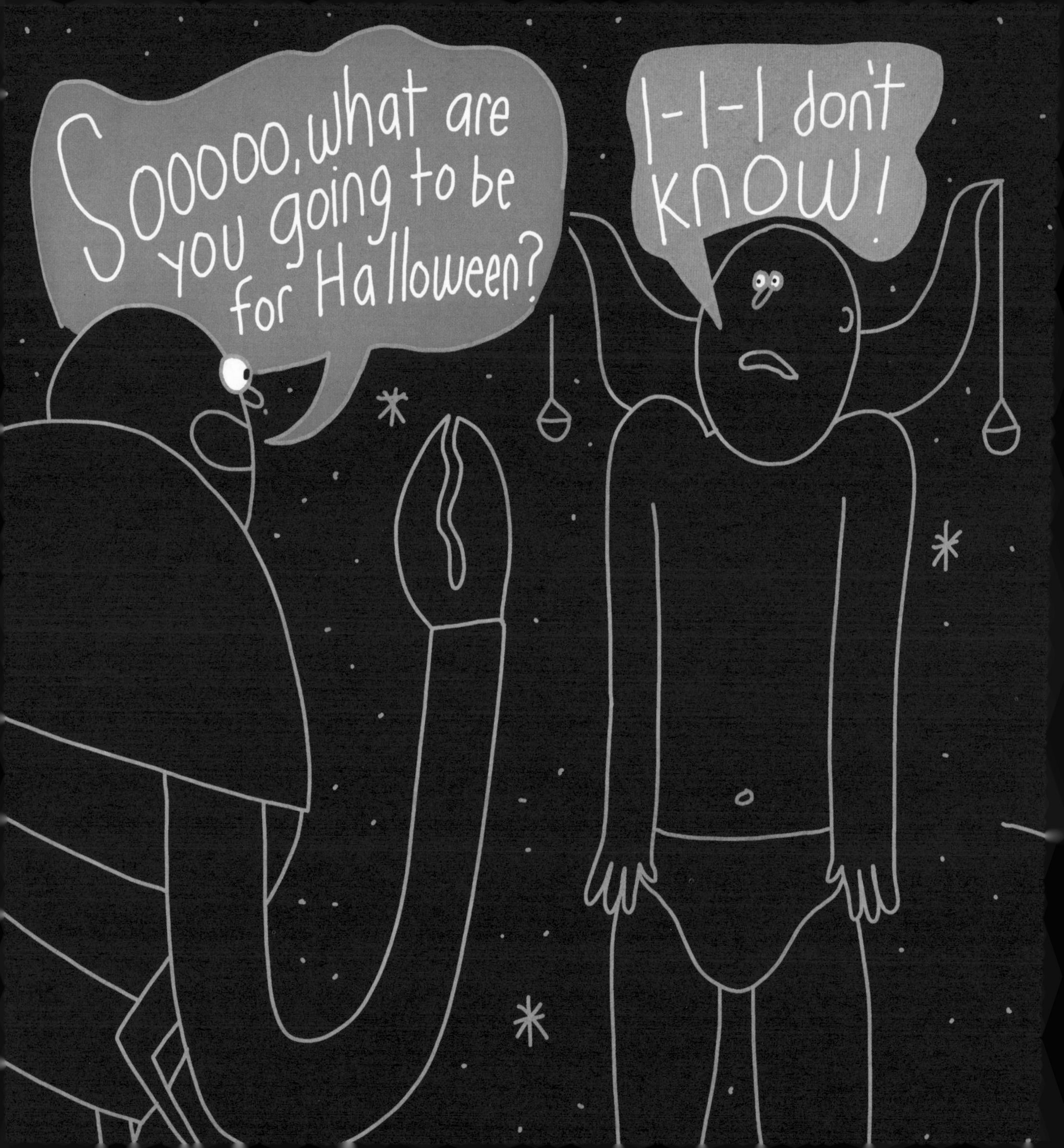
Sooooo, what are you going to be for Halloween?
I-I-I don't KNOW!

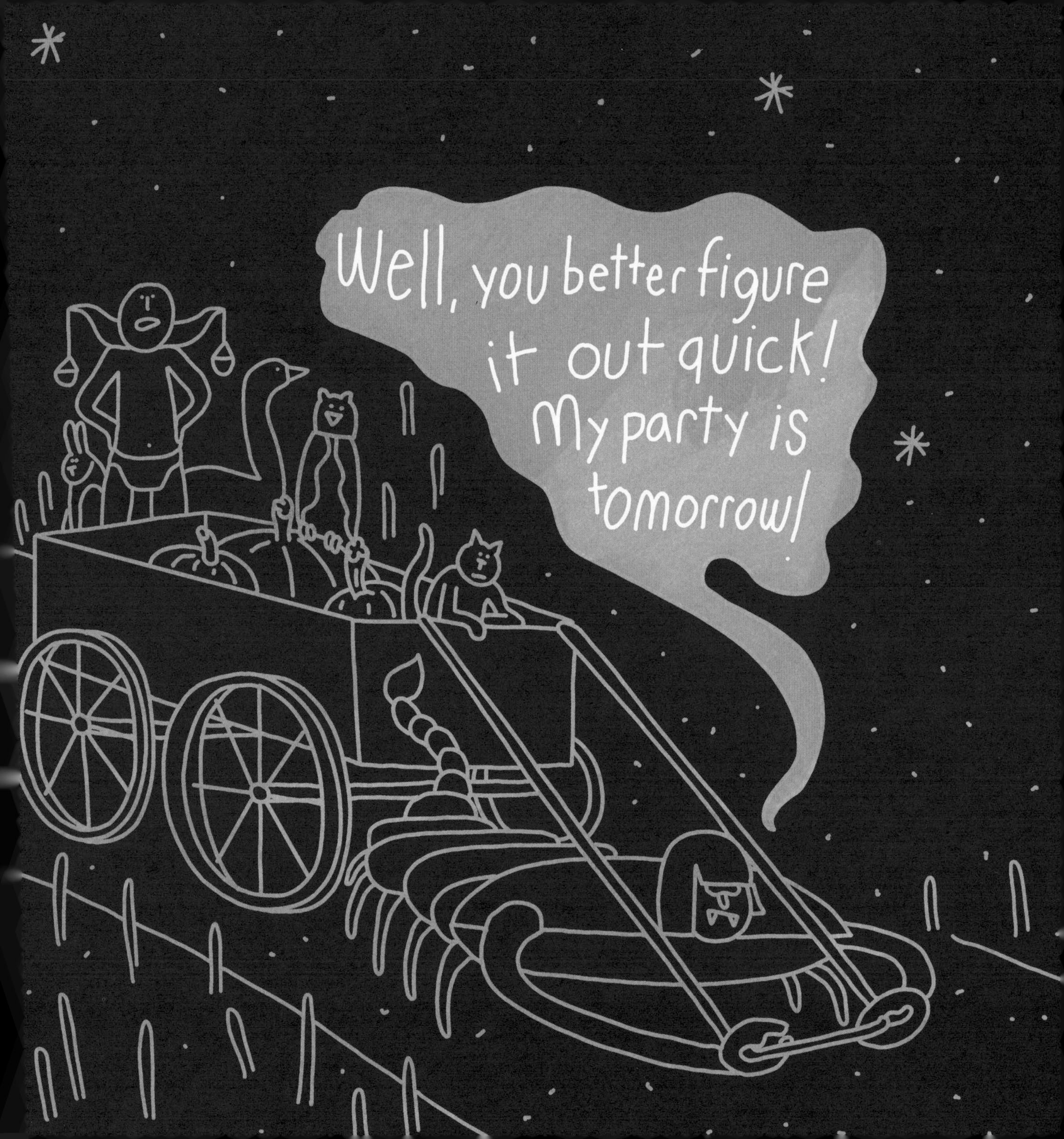
Well, you better figure it out quick! My party is tomorrow!

Hey Aquarius, are you going to Scorpio's Halloween party?
I sure am! You and me and Gemini should all go together! Air Sign POWER! I'm going to be an Intergalactic Alien Space Princess! what will you be?

Hey, Gemini. Do you know what you're going to be for Scorpio's Halloween party?
Yeah! I was torn between being a really sweet angel and an up-to-no-good devil. So I'm going to be both!

I could be Cinderella! I'll dance all night like I'm at a royal ball!

But then I'd have to marry a prince or
something. That sounds awful. Never mind.
Too bad, tho... I really wanted to wear a ball gown.

I'll be Coco Chanel! I'll be the chic-est kid at the party!

Forget it.
How could I be Coco Chanel?
I don't even speak French!
I guess I just wanted to wear all those pearls.

I'll be an Olympic athlete!

The big Winner!

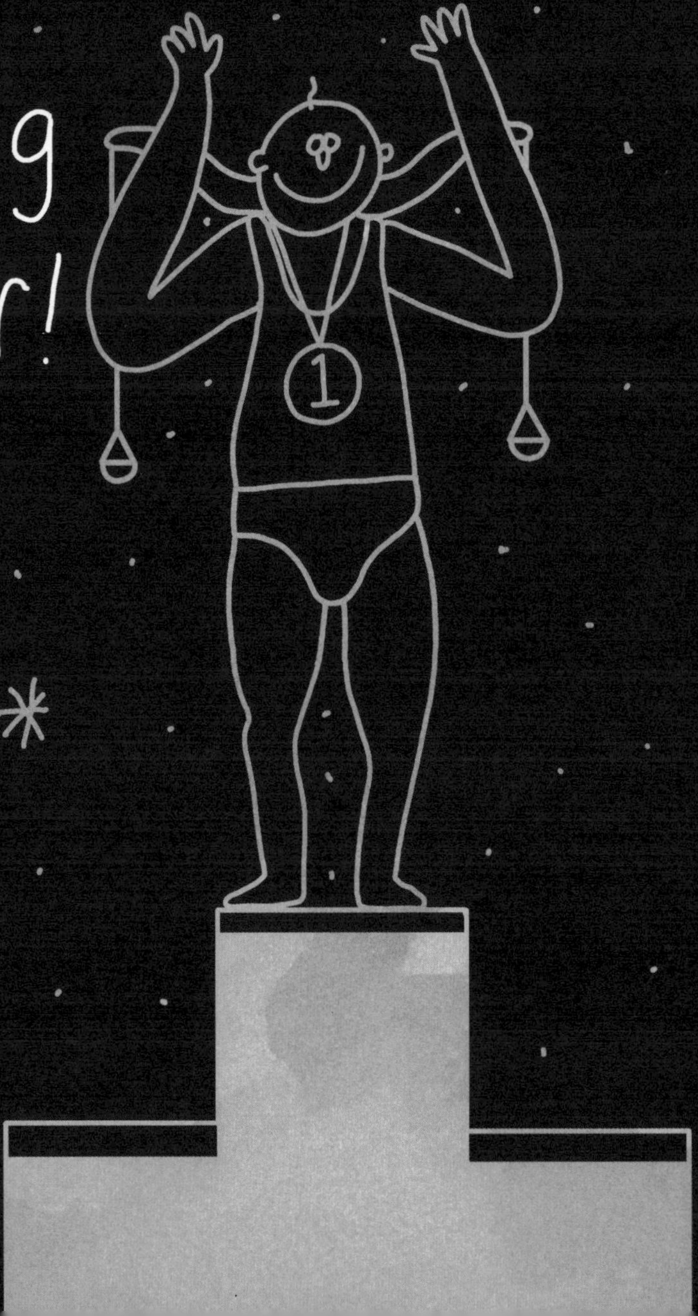

Bad idea. I'd be too cold in that little leotard. I think I just wanted to wear the shiny gold medal.

Of course! I'll be a fairy! What could
be more magical and fun?

But wait — fairies have to have glitter. And I hate glitter! It gets everywhere, even in my mouth! It's just not worth it.

This is the best idea! I wish I could be a mermaid all the time!

How do mermaids walk in these things? I'll break my neck in this costume. Bummer. I really wanted to wear the seashell crown.

I'll never find a costume! This is awful! I can't go to Scorpio's party. But Scorpio might be sad if I don't come! And Aquarius and Gemini—I'm supposed to go with them!

I don't want to hurt anyone's feelings.
I don't want to disappoint anyone.
I don't want anyone to know I can't choose
a Halloween costume! There's only
one thing to do... *LIE!*

*

There must have been something wrong with the mille-feuille. My tummy is totally terrible.

Aquarius,
I twisted my ankle getting into my excellent costume.
I can't walk.
I don't think I can make it to the party.
I'm so bummed.

Hey, Gemini. Bad news. I have an incredible fever. It must be like 400 degrees. I can't make it to the party.

What? Libra has a horrible fever! She needs to drink liquids and rest. I made her my tía's famous caldo de pollo. It's very healing.

All right! All right! I lied! I'm sorry! I didn't twist my ankle or get a fever or throw up my mille-feuille! I just couldn't decide what costume to wear, and it made me feel terrible.
I gave UP.

Um, at least I lied for a good reason. I didn't want you to feel bad, like I didn't want to spend time with you.
You can always tell us the truth, Libra. We would have been sad to not see you, but that's okay.

I don't know... I'm usually the helper. I didn't know I could ask for help.
Everyone needs help sometimes, Libra! That's what friends are for!

Now, get out of that bed, Libra!
We are going to help you create the most

Spectacular, phenomenal, majestic, Super-Libra Halloween costume ever!

I really wanted to wear my grandmother's pearls, and the medal I won in gymnastics, and my butterfly fairy wings, and the seashell crown my mermaid friend gave me...

Sorry I lied to you guys. Sometimes making a decision is so hard.

THE END...